# *Alligator at Saw Grass Road*

SMITHSONIAN'S BACKYARD

*For Laura, a loving daughter and kindred spirit*—J.H.

*I dedicate this book to my children, Chris and Camille, animal lovers and scientists of the future, with love*—L.A.

Book copyright © 2006 Trudy Corporation and the Smithsonian Institution, Washington, DC 20560.

Published by Soundprints, an imprint of Trudy Corporation, Norwalk, Connecticut.

Book design: Shields & Partners, Westport, CT
Book layout: Marcin D. Pilchowski
Editor: Barbie H. Schwaeber
Production Editor: Brian E. Giblin

First Edition 2006
10 9 8 7 6 5 4 3
Printed in Indonesia

*Acknowledgments:*
    Our very special thanks to Eli Bryant-Cavazos at the National Zoological Park, Smihsonian Institution for her curatorial review.
    Soundprints would like to thank Ellen Nanney and Katie Mann at the Smithsonian Institution's Office of Product Development and Licensing for their help in the creation of this book.

*Library of Congress Cataloging-in-Publication Data*

Halfmann, Janet.
    Alligator at Saw Grass road / by Janet Halfmann ; illustrated by Lori Anzalone. —1st ed.
    p. cm. — (Smithsonian's backyard)
    ISBN 1-59249-632-6 (hardcover book) — ISBN 1-59249-633-4 (pbk. book) —
    ISBN 1-59249-634-2 (micro book)
 1. American alligator—Juvenile literature.     I. Anzalone, Lori, ill. II. Title.

    QL666.C925H35 2006
    597.98'4—dc22
                                                    2006020682

# Alligator at Saw Grass Road

by Janet Halfmann
Illustrated by Lori Anzalone

Soundprints
Where Children Discover...

In early June, the red sun sets on the Florida Everglades. Something is happening in the grassy waters of the marsh behind the lone house at the end of Saw Grass Road. On a small tree island, Alligator prepares to build her nest.

With her strong jaws, she yanks saw grass, cattails and alligator flag out of the ground. She pushes these water plants, along with mud, into a mound under some trees.

Night after night, she adds to the big pile, until it is three feet tall—high enough to stay above water as summer rains flood the marsh.

When the nest is finished, Alligator climbs to the top and digs out a hollow with her scaly back feet. She lays thirty large white eggs with hard shells. She covers them with more plants to keep them safe and warm.

Now, Alligator slides down the bank into her gator hole to keep watch. This freshwater pond at the center of the tree island is special. Alligator dug it herself and weeds it constantly to keep it clean and deep.

During the winter when most of the shallow marsh dries up, her gator hole does not. Its life-giving waters attract fish, turtles, frogs, water snakes and birds from all over the glades. And that means plenty of food to keep Alligator's tummy full.

Alligator is a sneaky hunter. She floats in the water without making a ripple. Only her sparkling eyes and the tip of her nose poke out. A garfish thinks Alligator is a bumpy black log and swims close. In a flash, Alligator lunges. *Snap!* She crunches the fish in her toothy jaws and swallows it whole.

Alligator spends most of her time close to her nest. One night, as her catlike eyes peer from the rushes, a hungry raccoon finds the mound of hidden eggs. Alligator charges from the water, her huge mouth opened wide. *HISSSSSS!* The raccoon runs off to find food elsewhere.

Another time, when Alligator is distracted by a brown water snake, a female red-bellied turtle pushes right into the side of the nest. What does she want? She doesn't eat alligator eggs.

Inside the nest, the turtle lays twenty of her own eggs and then leaves. Now, without knowing it, Alligator will be guarding the turtle eggs, too.

All summer, the alligator eggs and the turtle eggs lie snug in the nest under the trees. The hot sun and the heat of the rotting plants keep the eggs warm. From time to time, Alligator drags her dripping body over the nest to keep it moist.

Then one hot, steamy night in the middle of August, tiny noises come from the nest. "*Umph, umph, umph.*" Alligator rushes over and gently claws off the hard top of the nest.

Inside, several little black and yellow alligators have broken open their shells. Now, the nine-inch-long babies wiggle free. So do several tiny red-bellied turtles!

Some baby alligators have trouble hatching, so Alligator helps out. One by one, she picks up the eggs in her huge jaws. She rolls them against the roof of her mouth with her tongue, gently cracking them. The baby gators squirm between her big, sharp teeth.

The eggs from the warm top of the nest hatch as males. Those from the cooler bottom hatch as females.

When all of the baby gators have hatched, Alligator starts picking them up in her mouth. She pulls her tongue down to form a special pouch where they can sit—ten at a time. Then she carries them to her gator hole.

The tiny turtles lie low until Alligator leaves the nest. Then they scamper to freedom. They head to the water, too, but are completely on their own.

Once all of the baby gators are in the water, Alligator grunts for them to follow her to a safe den hidden beneath the bank of the gator hole. The tired babies lie in the mud at the back of the den. Soon they fall asleep under Alligator's watchful eyes.

For the first few days, the babies live on the egg yolk in their bellies. Then they start hunting insects, frogs and tiny fish in the clear water of the gator hole.

But danger lurks everywhere. A great blue heron spots a baby exploring in some lily pads. "*Yurk, yurk, yurk!*" calls the frightened little one. Alligator swishes her powerful tail and splashes to the baby's side. The heron flies off and the baby is safe.

When the little gators aren't hunting or exploring, they sun themselves on top of Alligator's head and scramble over her back. They will stay near Alligator for two years or more. She will do everything she can to keep them safe as they grow up in the gator hole at the end of Saw Grass Road.

## About the Alligator

The American alligator, a reptile, is a member of the crocodile family. How do you tell an alligator from a crocodile? An alligator has a shorter, more rounded snout. And when an alligator's mouth is closed, only its top teeth show, while both the top and bottom teeth show in a crocodile.

American alligators live in the warm southeastern United States. They live primarily in freshwater swamps and marshes, such as the Florida Everglades, but also in rivers, lakes and smaller bodies of water.

Adult alligators, at ten to fourteen feet, are at the top of the food chain. They eat anything they can catch. They often hide in the water with only their eyes and noses showing, then snap up prey that comes near. They hunt mostly at night.

Alligators often dig gator holes, which are deeper than the rest of the marsh. Trees and other plants grow in the mud that the alligator piles up around the edges of these holes. Gator holes stay wet during dry times, providing much needed water for many animals and birds.

Male alligators attract females in the spring with rumbling bellows. After mating, a female is on her own. She builds a large, high nest of plants and mud for her eggs. She guards it and tears it open when the babies call. The mother carries her babies to water and protects them against their predators. Even so, few young survive their first year.

Young gators grow fast, about a foot a year. As they grow larger and stronger, their former predators become prey! Alligators in the wild can live thirty years or more.

## Glossary

*alligator flag:* Water plant with big flag-like leaves. It often grows around alligator holes.

*cattails:* Water plants with long, furry brown flower spikes.

*garfish:* Predator fish with long, narrow jaws and needle-like teeth

*gator hole:* A water hole made by an alligator. It will stay wet even during the dry season, providing vital water for alligators, fish, insects, snakes, crustaceans, turtles, birds and other animals.

*great blue heron:* Large wading bird that catches fish and other prey by sight.

*marsh:* Area of low, wet land where mostly grasses grow.

*saw grass:* A plant in the Florida Everglades, named for its leaves that resemble sharp teeth.

## Points of Interest in this Book

*pp. 6-13, 22-29:* water lily flower.
*pp. 8-9, 14-21, 24-25:* alligator nest.

*pp. 12-13:* garfish.
*pp. 16-17, 20-21, 24-25:* red-bellied turtle, turtle eggs.